BIKE LYFE

MAGAZINE

IN THIS ISSUE

2
DAME JACKSON

18
TAZ

23
Bike of the month

30
SOUND DR

38
COLLEGE MOM BIKER CHICK

Editorial
Lashonti Woods

Advertising
Tiffany McHenry

BIKELYFEMAG@GMAIL.COM

DAME
JACKSON

page 2

NAME: DAME JACKSON

Just a little about Dame

Name: Dame Jackson

Just a little about Dame I was born and raised in Oakland, Ca. When I was a toddler, I was diagnosed with tuberculosis (TB) Meningitis and was hospitalized for close to a year. That condition had me super attached to my mama because she was overprotective of me. When I was 12, my mama was shot and killed in West Oakland at 38.

From then on, I was raised by my grandma and built a closer relationship with my father, who lived across town. I was an honor roll student throughout middle school and high school.

Q: How did you become so passionate about photography?
A: Photography came easy because I've always loved pictures before I picked up a camera. I started collecting photos and got my first camera, a small sony digital camera. Then once I saw the big cameras, I eventually purchased one, and from there, I began to invest in more equipment, leading me to where I am today.

Q: How is your experience viewing the MC culture's life through a camera lens.
A: I got my first gig on the set in 2016. I didn't know anybody. All they knew was I was the guy taking pictures at the picture booth. But, as time passed, they started to pay attention to the man behind the lens (me), and I began to build bonds and repors with different clubs and people on the set. Like anything, there's a good and a not-so-good experience, but I push through it all.

Q: Why didn't you choose to ride a motorcycle?
A: Part of me wanted a motorcycle, but I invested my money in photography. I felt that I would never have time to ride it. But I'm not against getting one, maybe one day. So my saying comes from, "I'm just the Cameraman."

Q: What advice would you give another person wanting to create memories through a camera lens?
A: I would tell them to follow their passion and don't let anyone steer them in a different direction than they were not already trying to go. Everyone doesn't have the same vision for your passion, so their opinion shouldn't matter. Try it and fail first before you listen to someone who hasn't tried or who's not in your same field.

3RD ANNUAL WEEKEND
RARE BREED
M.C.
MOTOR
HARLEY-DAVIDSON
COMPANY
SACRAMENTO
Save The Date
SEPTEMBER 23RD-25TH 2022
TURNUP GRAPHICS 510-381-2029

WOMEN'S EMPOWERMENT RIDE

RIDE

KINDNESS

In collaboration with The World Kindness USA 25th year anniversary, we bring you Ride4Kindness to promote **#1voice4kindness.**

Ride4Kindness mission is to create tribute days of awareness in multiple states leading up to World Kindness Day, Nov 13, 2022, by asking bikers to ride from one destination to another within their state: or across the US, spreading smiles over miles.

Throughout history bikers have been spreading kindness over charity rides, events for causes, supporting businesses and by giving individuals in their community the strength of unity. Simple acts of kindness still make a world of difference, through one individual's eyes to global eyes.

Help break the barriers regarding bikers over the US and support ride4kindness to continue true acts of kindness bikers have participated in over history, and still do today.

"Simple acts of kindness can still make a world of difference, through one individual's eyes to global eyes."

To promote this event, we are introducing Augmented Reality (AR) via "ARcodes" into the mix of entertainment. How the "ARcode" works:

First: Open phone camera/ Place over code
Second: Tap link "arurl.co" / Allow Permission
Location
Third: Press "Start Here"/ Allow Permissions
Motion & Orientation
Camera
Four: Place Reticle to Experience AR Message

This code is the one stop scan that will keep you updated on all the latest information.

We encourage weekend riders, hardcore riders, adventure riders, BCs, and MCs to bring 100%. We welcome all to participate.

Stay Scanned In.

Augmented Reality Experiences brought to you by:

Salute2Kindness Awards 2022

Coming in November
A Week of Kindness!

Reno G

Q: What club are you in?
A: Hog Nutz MC

Q: What kind of Motorcycle do you have?
A: 2018 Harley Davidson Road king Special

Q: What's the furthest distance you have ridden?
A: Oakland, Ca to Phoenix AZ

Q: How did you get the name Reno G?
A: Reno is my family name. RIP to Spyke; however, he called me RENO G because my last name begins with a G.

Q: Is it easy to balance the set and home life?
A: Not Always. Balancing family events and MC events will always happen. But, you must choose what's most important to you and stand by your decision.

HOG NUTZ

HOG NUTZ

RENO G
HOG NUTZ

Q: How has Hog Nutz impacted your life?
A: These guys are my brothers. We all kicked it before becoming an MC and even kicked it when it's not MC-related, ATVs, UTVs, boats, you name it. They all one call or text away and email for the OGs, LOL.

Q: If you could change three things about the MC community, what would it be and why?
A: I would like to see more support from the out state club's annuals. It's more than California and Arizona bike sets. The clubs down south, Midwest, and east coast got a lot to offer. Incredible people who respect the set too. I would also like to see more fellowship with the OG MC clubs and the young MC. It's still a significant division of the generations. Some of the young cats don't respect those who paved the way. Then you got some OG's who don't put their arms around the youngsters and share the history.

Q: Is there any advice you would give someone who wants to join an MC club?
A: I say fellowship with club members outside of the MC set. Get to know who folks are and what they do day to day.

LADIES OF
SUBSTANCE

9TH
ANNUAL

AUGUST 5TH 2022
CIGARS, FEDORAS,
DENIM AND COGNAC

DOORS OPEN @ 8PM

ELKS LODGE

1020 ALABAMA ST VALLEJO CA

TURNUP
GRAPHICS
510-381-2029

IN THE MIX

360 PHOTOBOOTH

BY
TMP PHOTOGRAPHX

PRICE LIST

2 HOURS
3 HOURS

CONTACT US

415 - 758 - 3263 (DAME)
Tmpphotographx@gmail.com

GREAT FOR...

BIRTHDAY PARTIES - ANNIVERSARIES -
WEDDING - PRIVATE EVENTS -
CORPORATE EVENTS AND MORE!

$200
Per hour

BOOK US NOW!

PLEASE HAVE AT LEAST A 8X8 AREA

Name: P Dubb

How did you get interested in riding motorcycles?

My pop's used to take me for rides on his chopper at 12. That's how I got interested in motorcycles.

What kind of motorcycles do you ride?

I ride a 2017 Road Glide.

What's been your worst experience riding?

My worst experience was riding to Chicago a year ago, and I wasn't prepared for the cold weather.

P DUBB

Q: If you could change anything about the world of motorcycling, what would it be?
A: Absolutely nothing.

Q: Are you in a club?
A: No, I'm not in a club. I want to be in a club that rides their bike out of state function.

Q: How was your experience riding across the country?
A: It was terrific; I cant wait to do it again.

Q: What would you have done differently for your ride?
A: I would have done nothing different. Part of riding is dealing with whatever the world throws your way.

Q: What has been your best experience riding?
A: I like meeting other people who ride their motorcycles.

Q: What advice would you give someone wanting to ride a motorcycle?
A: If you have never ridden a bike before, my advice is not to.

WwwKrakenShoes.Com

SOUTHERN DESIRE PRESENTS

ALL FEMALE BIKERS SHOWDOWN

Buckles & Boots

OCT 15   12PM-8PM

$10 DONATION
WARREN FAIRGROUND
106 S JOHN C MOSS DRIVE, WARREN, AR

MUSIC BY

DJ JOCK

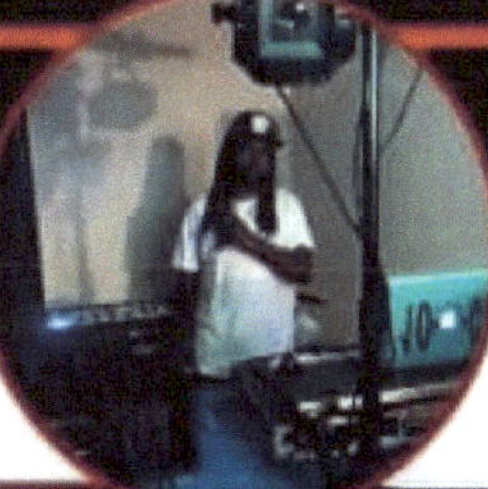

TROPHIES FOR BEST 2 AND
3 WHEEL BIKE AND
FURTHEST DISTANCE

FOR MORE INFO
CONTACT INFRARED AT
501-400-4214

VENDORS WILL BE ONSITE

NO LIMIT RIDERS NOR SOUTHERN DESIRE IS RESPONSIBLE FOR DAMAGED
OR STOLEN PROPERTY OR PERSONAL INJURY

TAZ

Location: Richmond, Ca
Club Name: Fugitives MC Richmond Chapter

Q: What kind of motorcycle do you ride?
A: Harley Davidson Electra Glide. I call her Queen B when we're acting up and Daisy blue when we're just cruising.

Q: What made you want to join an MC club?
A: I joined a club for the brother and sisterhood. I also join to give back to our community.

Q: When did you first begin to ride motorcycles?
A: I started riding last year in April 2021. I took the class and bought my first hog, and took off.

Q: What's been your best experience riding?
A: I like meeting new people. I've gained a few brothers. A female on a Harley is a conversation piece. Riding, to me, is a stress reliever. Buying my motorcycle was one of the best decisions I made for myself.

Q: What's been your worst experience riding?
A: That would be riding around a bunch of cars that are not watching out for motorcycles. The number one rule is never to get too comfortable and constantly watch your surroundings.

Q: Tell BLM about your first long-distance ride?
A: My first long-distance ride was to LA for our mother chapter annual. Just four months on the ground, I rode up front with the Prez. He talked a bunch of crap about me having tunnel vision every time we stopped. It was my first time riding side by side. I was focused on holding my side of the lane. I don't think I let my grips go once on that trip, and I probably didn't adjust my music.

Q: What advice do you give someone wanting to join a club?
A: Find a club that suits you. Hang around before you become a prospect, and don't rush the process when your prospecting. If you like to party, find a club that party. If you like to ride, find a club that rides hard. Some clubs want to give back. Just see what fits you so you will be happy. The brother/sisterhood is about family and loyalty among friends. It's the "Camaraderie" for me.

HATER-MAKERS SC
FRESNO
3RD Annual
AUGUST
5TH
2022
FEATURING:
MC/DJ DRE SNACKS
MASK ARE MANDATORY
PREZ & VP FREE
UNKNOWNS CLUBHOUSE 224 W. NAPA RD FRESNO CA

Name: Bouje'
Club: Queens Of Cali
Location: North Bay

Q: What made you join Queens of Cali?
A: The no-drama sisterhood attracted me because I am a Queen in my own way.

Q: What challenges have you faced being in an all-female club?
A: Just the connection mostly. I find most women have their guards up when connecting with new women. The loyalty and trust factor has to be gained. It takes time.

Q: What does your club look for in members?
A: In my opinion, grown women who want to be committed to a sisterhood and community services. Also, women who wants to be in the club for the right reasons. Not to chase men, even though men are a part of the set, but honestly, in it to build bonds with their club sisters.

Q: If you could change one thing about your group, what would it be?
A: More off-the-set get-togethers with my sisters.

Q: What is one thing in 2022 you will do differently in the group?
A: As a whole, regarding the set, I plan to do more as part of being in an SC is being more social with other SC clubs outside of Queens of Cali. Also, doing more walks at club functions to represent my club, Queens.

TRU
RYDERZ MC
MC
AUG. 19th - 20th
SAVE THE DATES

BIKE OF THE MONTH

Divas 2 Die 4 Bay Area MC
PRESIDENT

PATTY MELT

Q: What kind of motorcycle do you have?
A: 2020 HD Special, #1 Racer, Road Glide.

Q: What's the furthest you have ridden?
A: ATL

Q: Is it easy to balance the MC world and home life?
A: Balance is not what I call it, living simultaneously or parallel with my home and work life. There's no such thing as balance when this motorcycle lifestyle is not a style but your life. There no escaping that.

Q: What's your club name?
A: The infamous Divas 2 Die 4 organizations. Yes, we are an organization, not just a club. We have both MC/SC, and we are community advocates.

Q: If you could change three things about the MC community, what would it be and why?
A:

1) The money clubs make off of throwing multiple parties and events. The money attracts non-riders, but people with bikes are trying to capitalize on our culture. That's why pop-up clubs are throwing 4 to 5 events a year.

2) I want to see more Women MC clubs supporting SC club events. It continues to separate us if we don't get it out of our heads that we are not the same because of a motorcycle.

3) Last but not least. The most important one is to bring family picnics to the club. If you're in a club, the whole family is, or it won't work. Being on the set impacts everything you do and everyone in your life.

Q: HOW MANY MEMBERS DO YOU HAVE?
A: THAT'S NOT PUBLIC INFORMATION.

Q: AS A PRESIDENT, WHAT KEEPS YOU GOING WITH BUILDING YOUR CHAPTER?
A: WOMEN ON MOTORCYCLES ARE BADASSES, AND I LOVE THEIR ENERGY AND VIBE. I RIDE REGARDLESS OF WHO I AM WITH, BUT SEEING A GREAT GROUP OF WOMEN FLYING OUR CUTS IS THE MOST SIGNIFICANT HIGH YOU CAN GET. IT DISPLAYS UNITY AMONGST US AND PROVES THAT WOMEN CAN CREATE SOMETHING PHENOMENAL WITHOUT FIGHTING.

Q: WHAT IS YOUR VISION FOR 2022 WITH YOUR CHAPTER?
A: 2020 IS ALMOST OVER. SO I WANT TO USE THIS TIME TO EDUCATE, CREATE A TRANSPARENT SYSTEM AND DEVELOP TRANQUILITY.

Q: WHAT HAS BEEN YOUR BEST EXPERIENCE WHILE BUILDING YOUR CHAPTER?
A: GETTING TO KNOW WHAT WORKS AND DOESN'T WORK. I AM LEARNING MYSELF AND THE OTHER LADIES.

Q: WHAT HAS BEEN YOUR WORST EXPERIENCE WHILE BUILDING YOUR CHAPTER?
A: MIXING IN THE WRONG ENERGY IN A GROUP OF WOMEN ALREADY EXPERIENCING CHALLENGES WITHIN THEMSELVES AND HAVING TO DEAL WITH SOMEONE WHO ISN'T A FIT.

Q: WHAT IS ONE THING AS A CHAPTER YOU WOULD WANT TO SEE CHANGE ON THE SET?
A: I BELIEVE AS A CHAPTER, WE WOULD WANT TO SEE MORE ORGANIZED EVENTS THAT ADD VALUE TO THE INDIVIDUAL AND WOMEN TO RECEIVE JUST AS MUCH RESPECT AS THE FELLAS ON THE SET.

PATTY MELT

HEELS ON WHEELS SC
SACRAMENTO
BACK TO THE
90'S
16TH ANNUAL
DANCE
$15 Vested
Prez & Vp Free
$20 W/O Vest
FRIDAY
AUGUST 26TH 2022
Trophies For : Longest Distance , Deepest Mc , Deepest Sc
DJ CHI - TOWN IN THE MIXXX
DRE SNACKS ON THE MIC
TURNUP GRAPHICS
510-381-2029

BIRMINGHAM, AL
RARE BREED MC PRESENTS
September 22-25, 2022
Dirty Birds M.C
ANNUAL

Thurs. Sept. 22nd
Low Riders MC Hangnight
600 17th St.
Birmingham, AL 35218
8pm-12am

Fri. Sept. 23rd
Meet-N-Greet @ Da Nest
3421 27th St. N.
Birmingham, AL 35207
9pm-Until

Sat. Sept. 24th
Block Party @ Da Nest
3421 27th St. N.
Birmingham, AL 35207
1pm-5pm

Annual Party @ CLUB M
521 3rd Ave. W
Birmingham, AL 35203
9pm-2am
Trophies will be awarded...

$15/Advance
$20 @ Door

Host Hotel:
Home 2 Suites
3289 Lowery Pkwy
Fultondale, AL 35068
(205)407-4985
Code: Rare Breed

Contact info:
Scientific (334)220-2896
Train (205)478-5281
Badboy (205)586-9772

Overflow:
La Quinta Inn & Suites
1207 Boots Blvd
Fultondale, AL 35068
(205)949-8700
Code: Rare Breed

10 YEAR Aniversary
FRESNO
HEELS ON WHEELS
SAVE THE DATE
NOVEMBER | 18 2022

SOUND DR

page 30

SOUND DR

Name:
Chuck Thompson
Location:
Corona Ca

Q: Are you in a club?
A: Not in a club, but hang with all local clubs regularly. My cousin is the president of Black Knightz MC Big Ques.

Q: What kind of motorcycle do you ride?
A: Currently, I have a 2014 CVO road king converted to a Road Glide.

Q: When did you first begin to ride motorcycles?
A: I started riding mini bikes as a teenager, then on dirt bikes. I got my first street bike 2003 Yamaha R6. Then my first Harley in 2010 was a 2005 Road Glide. Then shortly after, I started selling Harley's at Riverside Harley. In 2016 I got a 2015 Road glide.

Q: Tell BLM about your first long-distance ride?
A: My first long-distance ride was from LA to Phoenix, AZ. Road with the club 110 to the end as a civilian rider, and we did 110 from the time we got on the highway till we got off. This was also my first time riding in heavy wind.

Q: Do you have any advice for someone wanting to ride a bike?
A: My advice for new riders is to make sure this is something you really want to do in your heart. Also, getting a Harley is addictive. It's a lifestyle, not just owning/riding a motorcycle. Make sure your spouse/significant other is ok with your decision to want to come to hang out and understand you will spend a lot of time with your new passion. And lastly, respect the machine, ride aggressively, paying attention to your surroundings.

BIKE LYFE
MAGAZINE

ADVERTISE
YOUR

- SERVICE
- PRODUCTS
- EVENTS
- BIKE

Email

bikelyfemag@gmail.com

@Bikelyfemag

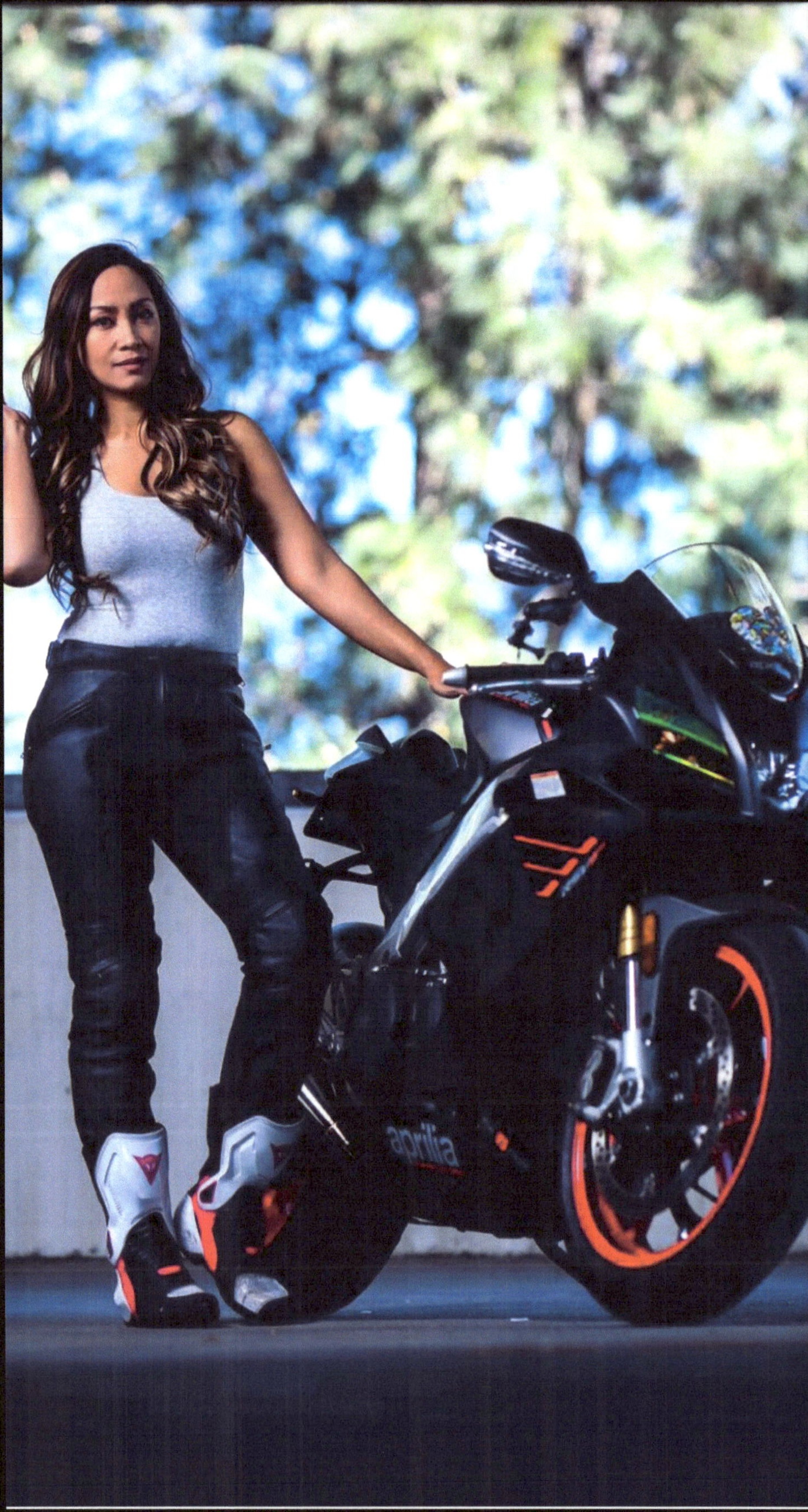

FANNIE DETAIL

BONAFIDE RIDERS
MC CLUB

Q: What kind of motorcycle do you ride?
A: Street Glide

Q: Is it easy to balance the set and home life?
A: Yes, it is because family is always first.

Q: If you could change three things about the MC community, what would it be and why?
A: One is getting it back to fun and supporting each other more. Secondly is having members ride their bikes more than mandatories. Last but not least is making members earn their patch instead of just giving it to them quickly.

Q: Is there any advice you would give someone who wants to join an MC club?
A: Take your time before you pick a club. Make sure it's a good fit for you.

Gentlemen MC Weekend

BM GRUMPY
480 254 6857

BM THREAT
313 282 6879

BM 4G
480 809 1995

AUGUST 11,12,13
13 S. 36st Phoenix

SONESTA SELECT
601 S ASH AVE
TEMPE AZ 85281
SINGLE/DOUBLE
$99 PER NIGHT

POOL
PARTY
2-5
SATURDAY

TROPHIES
BIGGEST MC
BIGGEST FEMALE MC
BIGGEST CO-ED MC
BIGGEST SC
FARTHEST TRAVELED

RARE BREED MC BATON ROUGE CHAPTER
BOOTS & JEANS
10/29/22
SAVE THE DATE

Dallas
CHAPTER

KINGZ OF THE SOUTH
M.C.
MOTOR
HARLEY-DAVIDSON
CYCLES

SAVE
THE
DATE

CROWNING
THE
CITY II
AUGUST 11-14, 2022

BIKE LYFE

#1 MAGAZINE

AVAILABLE ON
amazon

WE DO : BUSINESS ADS, CLUB INTERVIEWS, PARTY FLYERS ETC

(LET US HELP YOU BUILD YOUR BRAND AND GET YOUR BUSINESS OUT THERE)

ADS SPACE AVAILABLE

ARE YOU READY TO BE IN THE NEXT ISSUE OF THE BIKE LYFE MAGAZINE ????

CONTACT US @

EMAIL: Thuzzlmc@gmail.com

FACEBOOK: Tiffany Lynette

INSTAGRAM: t_huzzlmc

TURNUP GRAPHICS

510-381-2029

COLLEGE MOM BIKER CHICK

I'm a college Mom Biker Chick. I am a motorcycle enthusiast from the Bay Area in California. I have been riding since the summer of 2016. I have absolutely no regrets.

I currently ride a 2016 Road Glide and want to cordially invite you all on my journey as I navigate through this Bike life as a first-generation college student and mother. Along the way, I aspire to encourage and empower all to be their authentic selves and even mount up on a motorcycle. I am looking forward to generating more inclusion for women in the world of motorcycles.

Q: How did you get interested in riding motorcycles?
A: I genuinely believe it was genetically in me to ride motorcycles. I have a grandfather who was riding coast to coast with his buddies until 5years ago. My mom also loves motorcycles, but she never learned how to ride.

Q: What's been your worst experience riding?
A: My worst experience riding is not riding. Yes, I have been in motorcycle accidents caused by drunk drivers before, even been on the side of the highway solo. However, not riding is what hurts me the most.

I BELIEVE I AM LEADING
FOR EXAMPLE, THROUGH ADVOCATING
AND HOSTING MORE RIDES TO
ENCOURAGE MORE RIDING AND
FELLOWSHIP AMONG ALL RIDERS.

Hard Riders
MC
DALLAS, TEXAS

2ND ANNIVERSARY
APRIL 1 & 2, 2022

$15 PRE-SALE / $20 @ THE DOOR

HOST HOTEL: Hampton Inn & Suites
Duncanville Dallas
202 East Interstate Hwy 20
Duncanville, TX • 469-868-6481

APRIL 1, 2022 • MEET & GREET
Attche' Cigar Lounge
4099 W. Camp Wisdom Rd. • Dallas, TX
8pm - 2am

COME HANG WITH THE FLAME

APRIL 2, 2022 • DAY PARTY
Texas Harley-Davidson
1 Texas Harley Way • Bedford, TX
12pm - 5pm
TEXAS HARLEY

APRIL 2, 2022 • ANNUAL PARTY
White Diamonds
3906 W. Camp Wisdom Rd. • Dallas, TX
9pm - Until
REACH OUT TO ANY MEMBER WITH ANY QUESTIONS

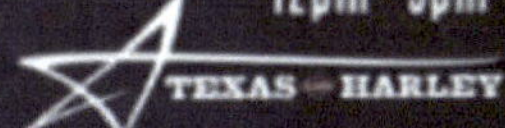

BOOT RAFFLE
$20 A TICKET • DRAWING WILL BE ON APRIL 2, 2022 AT ANNUAL PARTY
GET YOUR VERY OWN PAIR OF CUSTOM BOOTS
BY JESSE'S BOOTS 1960 AT VALUE OF $1,200
GET YOUR TICKETS FROM ANY HARD RIDER OF THE DALLAS CHAPTER

JESSE
BOOTS